D1150375

THE

Joan Aiken is the author of nearly 100 books for children and adults, including many that are considered modern classics. Her best-sellers include *The Wolves of Willoughby Chase, Black Hearts in Battersea, Go Saddle the Sea, Arabel's Raven* and *A Necklace of Raindrops*. She has won the Guardian Children's Book Award, the Kate Greenaway Medal and been nominated for the Carnegie Medal. She lives in Sussex.

'As thrilling and unsettling as you'd expect from this author'
The Observer

'Aiken writes superbly chilling stories . . . this is one of her best'
Independent on Sunday

'Aiken is on spine-tingling form . . . this tautly written story packs a punch and will grip those . . . who are not easily spooked'
Times Educational Supplement

'A tense, strangely disturbing story'
The Parent's Guide

The Scream

Joan Aiken

Illustrated by Ian Andrew

MACMILLAN CHILDREN'S BOOKS

First published 2002 by Macmillan Children's Books
a division of Macmillan Publishers Limited
20 New Wharf Road, London N1 9RR
Basingstoke and Oxford
www.panmacmillan.com

Associated companies throughout the world

ISBN 0 330 39703 6

3 5 7 9 8 6 4 2

A CIP catalogue record for this book is available from
the British Library.

Phototypeset by Intype London Ltd
Printed and bound in Great Britain by
Mackays of Chatham plc, Chatham, Kent

*To Charles and Hilary Schlessiger who gave me
the screaming cushion*

1

The Island

My sister Lu-Lyn was a disaster area. Total. How did it happen? First, from as early as I can remember, she wanted to go and live with Gran.

'Why? Why do you want to?' I can remember Mum saying. 'Give me one sensible reason. David doesn't want to. Why should you?'

'Because Gran lives on the island. David's only a boy. And he's never been there.'

It was an island called Muckle Burra. Far north of the north tip of Scotland. Lu-Lyn was born there. But then Mum and Dad had to move because of his job. Lu-Lyn had been back, three times since, to stay with Gran. She had never forgotten a single minute of any of those visits.

'It's the only place where I ever want to live.'

'But it takes days and days to get there from almost anywhere,' Mum pointed out. 'That's why Dad had to leave. What about your schooling? What about your ballet classes?'

Of course, the ballet classes were a strong argument. And another, a clincher, was that, by and by, Gran herself had to leave the island.

'Why? *Why*?' Lu-Lyn wanted to know.

'The Department of Health are shifting everybody who lives on Muckle Burra.' (There were only forty people altogether.)

'Why are they shifting them? How can they make people leave their homes?'

'They pay compensation. People can get bigger, more modern houses on the mainland.'

'I wouldn't leave *my* home. Not if it was a lovely white cottage with a garden like Gran's.'

'I suppose, in the end, they *have* to go,' sighed Dad. He didn't sound happy about it. He too had been born in that cottage. 'There's no power. No services. No way of getting to the mainland. Unless you have your own boat.'

'I'd have my own boat.'

Lu-Lyn drew endless pictures of the island, of

2

Gran's cottage, of the garden, of the flowers she would plant when she went back to live with Gran, of the boat she would build, of the fish she would catch. Sometimes the island was covered with trees.

'But it isn't like that. It's bare and grassy,' Dad argued.

'There are trees when I dream about it. Sometimes.'

'Anyway, it's no good. You can't live there. They are making the people leave.'

'Why? *Why?*'

'They are going to poison the island.'

'*Poison* the *island*? That's wicked!'

'For a scientific experiment. They want to find out what happens to the soil, and the animals, and the birds, and the fish, I suppose.'

'That's horrible!'

It did seem so. Perhaps that is what started all the trouble.

'A lot of people think that way,' said Dad. 'There have been protests.'

Gran was not among the protesters. She had a very calm nature. She shrugged and packed up her scanty belongings and moved to a tenth-floor flat in a tower-block in Kirkbrae near us on the mainland.

You got a great view from the top of her block

on a clear day. First, the grimy outskirts of Kirkbrae – factory roofs, cranes, derricks and chimneys – then the masts and funnels of ships, the river estuary, the Druidh Firth, then the rugged outlines of northern islands across the channel, Burra, Stour, Camsoe, Mink Ness – beyond them the Atlantic, away to the west.

Lu-Lyn still wanted to go and live with Gran, and in the end she got her way. But that was because Mum and Dad were killed in a motorway pile-up. I had to go along too, in my wheelchair. Luckily there were lifts at Chateau Mansions.

A queer thing: Lu-Lyn was homesick. Not for our own home. For the island where she had been born, which she had visited three times in her life. I used to hear her crying about it at night. Never in the daytime. And she went on drawing pictures of it. The island was her only friend, it seemed.

What did Lu-Lyn look like? The kind of doll you'd win at a fairground stall by landing three hoops over a bottle – curly, butter-coloured hair, round bluebell eyes, and a grin she could switch on and off like a blowtorch. She never wasted her grin, never switched it on unless she wanted you to do something for her. Never.

I have to say, Lu-Lyn and Gran got on well together. Surprisingly, because they seemed very different. Gran was thin and spare and old and cobwebby. And her eyes drilled through you like lasers. But she and Lu-Lyn both felt the same way about the island. It was important to them in a way I didn't understand at that time. Now I do.

Gran and Lu-Lyn saw eye-to-eye about *one* important thing, which was that Lu-Lyn should always have her own way . . .

In her young days, Gran had been a painter. Among other things. She did pictures of birds and wild creatures in queer places – seagulls in sinks, rats poking their snouts out of bookshelves, naked people wandering in forests. Once, Gran had been quite famous. Some of her queer bird and beast pictures hung on the walls of her flat, and that, maybe, was why she let Lu-Lyn have a pigeon of her own, though pets weren't allowed in Chateau Mansions.

Lu-Lyn's pigeon, Henry, used to fly in through the bathroom window, which always had to be kept open, and he perched on the end of Lu-Lyn's bed. He lived on corn, which got scattered all over. You'd think there would have been mice – but there were not. He dropped messes on the floor and he woke us at half-five every morning, roo-cooing like a cop car. And of course the bathroom was always freezing.

Gran had another picture, as well as those she'd done herself, and this showed a person screaming.

It was not the original, but a copy. The picture was a famous one, Gran told us, by a painter called Munch, who's dead now. (You don't say that name *Munch* to rhyme with lunch, but Moonck, like the word moon with a 'k' in it.) The picture shows this person, a girl I think, letting out a screech of total fright, hands up by her face, jaw dropped right down. It makes your bones prickle, just to look at her. You ask yourself what in the world she has just seen, close to her, a vampire or a charging grizzly, or a hungry dinosaur; and you wonder what is going to happen to her the very next minute.

Gran must have really liked that picture, for she had two spin-offs from it in her flat as well – a cushion with the horror-struck face printed on one side, which let out a shrill scream if you sat down on it, and an alarm clock. The clock had the face, with numbers faintly showing through, and its alarm, when wound, gave the same screeching wail that would freeze the blood right down to your fingernails.

'Where did you get them, Gran?' I asked her one time.

'Oh,' she said absently, 'people on the island gave them to me because they knew I liked them. As payment.'

'Payment for what, Gran?'

'Ridding their homes of rats.'

That answer really threw me. Gran seemed such a quiet, mild old body. *Rats?* How could she possibly do that?

I tried to imagine her, in her flowered cotton dress and shopping bag, going to people's houses and calling the rats out, like a Pied Piper. But my imagination fell down on the job.

'How did you do it, Gran?'

'One way or another . . .' She wasn't going to tell me. 'It's in the family,' she said vaguely. Her thin lips folded tightly. 'Girls, mainly,' she added. Being a boy – or being in a wheelchair – seemed to cut me off from something that Gran, and perhaps Lu-Lyn, knew without being told. I knew it would be no use asking any more questions.

Gran never used her Munch alarm clock. She hardly seemed to need sleep at all. But Lu-Lyn used to wind the alarm now and then, and set it for odd times, just to give us a fright. Which it did, every time. Luckily the neighbours complained if she did it too often.

2

The Tree

Going to school bored Lu-Lyn. Utterly. Ballet-type dancing was all she cared about. She had won plenty of prizes before Dad and Mum got killed. And Gran went on paying for her to have special classes.

'It's good to have two strings to one's bow,' she said once, which surprised me. For what other string did Lu-Lyn have?

Maybe she *was* good at dancing. I'm no judge. Maybe it wasn't just her butter-coloured curls and her 'see what a darling little thing I am' expression that got her to the top in all those festivals and competitions.

She worked hard, I'll say that.

Gran had a balcony outside her tenth-floor window, just big enough to hold two chairs and a coffee table. Lu-Lyn used to practise out there. She'd put a tape on the player and work for hours on end, with Henry the pigeon sitting beside her on the balustrade.

Down below was a little park.

Gran told us that the builders who'd put up Chateau Mansions and Castle Heights and Grange Towers and Fortress Manor would have liked to build a fifth block, but they weren't allowed. Believe it or not, the tallest tree in the country grew on that spot and, of course, it was protected. The tree was a fir, two hundred and thirteen feet three inches high – a miserable, moth-eaten spindly bit of vegetation, *I* thought it was. Maybe it had used up all its strength, growing so high. But Lu-Lyn quite liked it.

'It's the tallest tree in the land, and *I'm* going to be the best dancer in the country. My name will be in all the books,' she'd say, and she'd get out there on the terrace, clutching the rail, banging one leg against the other, five hundred times each side, looking at the tree sometimes in a neighbourly way.

I wondered if Gran had ever planned to be the best painter in the land?

Gran told us that the tree was left over from a forest that covered the whole country, years or centuries ago, before people built houses and cut down trees. And under the sea, too, millenniums back, when the big land-masses were joined together, there had been forests everywhere.

At the time I'm remembering, Lu-Lyn was practising for a school cabaret that was always held at the end of the autumn term. She'd made up her own dance for the show.

OK, you've guessed. Her dance was going to be called The Scream.

She'd found a piece of music, *The Banshee's Exile*, and she played this over and over while she practised. She found it in a collection, *Music from the Northern Isles*, by a composer called Ronald Ranuldsen.

'What's a banshee?' I asked Gran.

'A spirit woman who wails outside the windows when someone's going to die.'

'But why should she be exiled?'

'Because her place has been taken from her. Or her life.'

That was all Gran would say.

The terrace was not big enough for Lu-Lyn's dance; she had to work at that in any place she could make use of, a corner of the School Hall or the Ladies' Institute (when the ladies weren't using it) or, when the weather was fine, the bit of sooty grass in the park under the tallest tree.

But she was not too keen on the park because people used to stop and watch her, and she hated being watched.

Also there were three boys who were her enemies, and if they got to know that she was out there practising, they'd come along and stare and snigger and shout rude remarks.

She couldn't stand that. Or them.

Their names were Bry and Mack and Orrin.

Lu-Lyn once saw them push a car into the river. She told a cop – which got them into a lot of trouble.

'Well, I had to tell someone, didn't I?' she said later to Gran. 'There might have been a person in that car. Or a dog. I hate cruelty to animals.'

Gran pressed her thin lips together.

'Sometimes animals have to be drowned,' she said. 'When there are too many of them.'

'I think there are too many boys!' said Lu-Lyn.

I thought about rats on the island of Muckle Burra. I wondered if they were all poisoned now. And the rabbits, and the roe deer? It's really queer to think of a whole island being poisoned.

There had been no live creature in that car,

which was an old derelict in the corner of the car park. But, after that, every time a car was stolen, or vandalized, the cops tended to pounce on those three boys. Cops found them a natural target. So, of course, the boys had it in for Lu-Lyn.

One time, when they were under suspicion of dropping bricks from a railway footbridge on to the Glasgow express – the driver was in hospital for a year – the boys had a notion that it was Lu-Lyn who had shopped them.

That case never came to court, as nothing was ever proved.

But, a week after that, answering a ring at the bell, Lu-Lyn found Henry, her pigeon, lying on the doormat with all his feathers pulled out and his neck wrung.

Have you ever seen a bald pigeon? A wretched sight, he was.

Lu-Lyn was never one to cry or carry on. Not in public. After the accident that killed Mum and Dad she was perfectly calm. She did turn white at the sight of Henry – as white as the paper I'm writing on – and she said to Gran, 'Look what's been done to Henry.'

'Oh my word!' said Gran. That was all she ever said, when things went wrong.

But she helped Lu-Lyn bury Henry's remains.

They did it at midnight, a time when no one would be about to say they were contravening the park restrictions, under the tall fir tree outside Gran's window.

Gran asked Lu-Lyn if she'd like another pigeon. But she said no, maybe the same thing would happen again.

3

The Letter

I heard them talking about it one time when I was working on an algebra assignment. Their voices were very quiet. But I have sharp ears. I can hear bats squeak when they first come out in the twilight.

'If your aunt Arbel hadn't died . . .' Gran was saying.

'But that was a long time ago!'

'Time makes no difference at all.'

'Is the power always passed on? Is there always

a girl in the family? Suppose there isn't? Or suppose she should die? Would a boy do?'

A jet passed screaming overhead, so I missed Gran's next words.

'. . . never happened on the island,' Gran was saying when I caught her again.

'Shall we ever get back there, Gran, do you think?' Lu-Lyn's voice was very sad.

'No use planning on it. Not unless I get a message.' Gran, unusually for her, sounded doubtful.

'But what can I do about those three boys?'

'You *could* send them a letter.' Gran went on, a bit reluctantly, I thought. 'That's one of the ways I used to deal with vermin. Pin the paper to a post, where they can see it, or slip it in where they live.'

'Can rats read?'

'Ach, I don't mean that kind of letter. Not written words. Just a sheet of black paper. You breathe on it before you fold it. That fixes your thought on the paper. Like a rune, it is.'

'*Breathe* on it?' Lu-Lyn said curiously.

'That's the way we did it on Burra – your great-great gran, and her mother, and hers, going far, far back. That's how they got rid of riffraff, or things that got in the wrong place. And another thing – it drains the verjuice out of *you*. It's not

15

canny to be full of bitterness and have poison running up and down your veins.'

Whether Lu-Lyn understood this, or believed it, I don't know. But later I saw her busy with sheets of paper which she had painted black.

Gran was quite right, I thought. There was a lot of acid in Lu-Lyn, under the sugar sweetness that she kept for strangers.

Two of the three boys, Lu-Lyn's enemies, lived in our block. All Lu-Lyn had to do was go up a couple of floors and slip the letters under the door. The third one needed a stamp and a postbox: Bry Bateman lived over on the other side of town.

Why did the thing work on him first?

If you believe in it, that is.

Actually Lu-Lyn gave Bry's letter to me to post on my way to school, and I dropped it in the river as we crossed the bridge. Benjy, who pushed my wheelchair, said, 'What's that?' and I said, 'An overdue competition entry.' I thought he gave me a queer look.

Now I believe that, even dropped in the river, it got there somehow. Water conducts electricity, doesn't it? Maybe it conducts ill-wishes too.

Bry, good at football, was in the town junior XI and, in the following Saturday's match against Crossgates, he got kicked in the head and lost his sight. Went blind.

*

16

At St Martha's Hospital they couldn't say whether it would be permanent or not; just have to keep hoping, they said.

Lu-Lyn's thoughts about what happened to Bry she kept to herself; unless she talked about it to Gran.

After the loss of Henry she was in a queer mood. Silent, and just nibbling at her meals, not taking enough to keep a sparrow alive, Gran said. Pale as wax. Even her hair turned pale; from butter-colour it faded to a whitish yellow, the colour of lemon pith.

The only thing she thought about was her dance. The Scream. She worked at it all the hours she had.

I had seen that dance so often that I could have done it myself (if I could dance) because Lu-Lyn needed me at hand to keep restarting the tape, *The Banshee's Exile.*

How the dance went: she's alone in a wood, this young girl, having a nice time, picking nuts or berries or flowers, listening to birds et cetera, doing whatever you do in woods; and then evening comes, the light dims, and she reckons it's time to go home. And she starts back along the way to town.

That's when she sees whatever it is – first a long way off, she can hardly believe it, then coming

17

closer and closer. She looks either side of the track – there's no escape. The way home won't do, she can't run fast enough, for the thing, whatever it is, must be *huge*. You can tell that by the way she stares – up, down, from side to side. So huge that it could catch her in one enormous leap.

I read once about a creature they have in the forests of Canada, they call it the Wendigo. It has huge fiery feet and it goes hopping through the trees, or high above the tops of the trees, in mile-long leaps, and then it picks you up, that's the end of you, it drags you along as a hawk might drag a dangling rabbit, with its feet scraping along the ground. If you get picked up and dragged along by the Wendigo your feet get worn right off, right back to the ankle-bones.

Maybe some creature like the Wendigo is what Munch's screamer sees.

(Or that is what I thought at that time.)

Weeks went by and now it was nearly time for the school cabaret. It's always held on a Saturday evening, in the school hall, which has a stage at one end. Lu-Lyn had only one chance to practise on that stage, for it was used all day long in various ways, school meetings and drama groups and choir practice and parent-teacher evenings and after-school activities. So she was nervous about it. The one time she had a try-out there she

18

told me to bring a measuring-tape and a piece of chalk, as well as the tape recorder.

'What's the chalk for?'

'For my three leaps.'

How her dance ended: when this girl sees the Whatever-it-is coming at her, the only thing she can do is to go backward. And she does that in three terrific leaps, right across the stage.

Lu-Lyn told me once that a very famous ballet dancer, his name was something like Minksy or Pinsky – no, Nijinsky, that's it, Nijinsky – this fellow was such an acrobat that he was able to hold himself up in the air for a few seconds at the top of his leap. You could actually see him hover in mid-air. Well, Lu-Lyn wanted to be able to do that, it was her chief wish. And when she took those three terrific backward jumps, I almost believed that she had brought it off. She seemed to go up and then hang, like a yo-yo from somebody's finger, before the downward curve of the vault took her back to the ground.

And to do it *backward*! That was really something!

I didn't *like* my sister Lu-Lyn – never could, never would. For one thing, she didn't like me. But I did have to respect her for her one-track wish to go on and win, and be the best there was.

You know that piece of nursery magic we had

when we were very small kids? Wishing on a star, the first one you see at dusk. 'Star light, star bright. First star I see tonight.' Well, I still use that, only I do it at the other end of the twenty-four hours. I wake early in the morning before other people are up. It used to be Henry the pigeon who woke me so early and I've never shed the habit. At the time, the time of Lu-Lyn's dance, just around then, the end of the autumn term, a big full moon used to shine in the bathroom window, which faced south-east, where the sun would later pop up; and often, to the right of the moon, there would be just this one star left over from all the rest, very bright: Venus, our geography teacher told us its name was. The moon would be all worn out, pale as a cream cheese, but Venus was dazzling bright.

So: 'Star light, star bright, *last* star I'll see tonight, let my sister Lu-Lyn win the prize!' Venus ought to help, she must have been a girl herself once.

You see, the cabaret was also a competition, the act that the audience voted as the best was awarded a prize, which was a free term at a dance and drama college. You can guess how much my sister Lu-Lyn was set on that.

Our school hall is a kind of spooky place to be in when it's empty and you're all alone there. That's because it hardly ever *is* empty, so it seems unnatural, like seeing an audience watching a play without any actors, or a bus rolling along without a driver in the driving seat. It's dusty and chilly, and dark without all the lights on, and there's a strong, sour smell of wet clothes and muddy fibre matting and dust.

There's a piano down below the stage for the school song – 'Stand up, Stand up for ever, we'll all stand together' – and I played chopsticks on the piano while Lu-Lyn was taking off her raincoat and putting on her dancing shoes.

'*Don't* do that!' she said at once.

'Why not?'

'Someone might hear.'

'What difference does that make? You got permission to use the stage from four to five. You can do as you like. No one has the right to turn us out.'

'I didn't get permission to play chopsticks.'

This surprised me a bit. It was not like Lu-Lyn, who normally didn't give a rap for anybody's permission.

'Put on the tape,' she said then. 'I want to hear how it sounds in here. Put it on loud.'

4

The Dance

I put on *The Banshee's Exile* tape. It is very, very sad.

It sounded really weird – if there were any actual banshees lurking about, it must have made them feel pretty second-rate. The hall had screens at the back and up in the roof to improve the acoustics, and echoes from the long drawn-out wailing music seemed to come from every corner. A couple of bats who'd taken up residence on a rafter were disturbed and came fluttering down, squeaking disapproval, and a loose lightbulb dropped away from its fitting and smashed to the ground.

And I thought I heard somebody let out a gasp of fright from the rear of the hall where there were racks for hanging raincoats.

'What was that?' I said.

'Nothing, nothing!' said Lu-Lyn sharply, and she hopped up on to the stage.

She was wearing her costume for the dance. Gran had helped her with it. It was an all-over opaque body-stocking, in a leafy, ripply pattern of dark brown and black. Only her face was uncovered and it looked unnaturally white by contrast. Maybe she had whitened it.

The stage was dim, with just one overhead greenish strip light. Although I was so close I could only just see Lu-Lyn flitting about, doing her girl-alone-in-the-woods routine. Her face looked as if it were there on its own, like a white balloon floating around.

'It's a shame you can't have a backdrop of trees,' I said. 'That would make it seem even more real.'

Lu-Lyn didn't answer, took no notice. But I was bound to admit that, as she danced, she did somehow make you think of a wood, with big trees all round her, and forest stretching a long way off in every direction. Joining two continents, perhaps.

23

'Aren't there *any* woods on Muckle Burra?' I asked Gran once. But she said, no.

'No part of the island is more than two-and-a-half miles from the sea. Salt spray stops the growth of big trees. But,' said Gran, 'all those islands were once part of a big land area long ago all joined together. They have found fossilized forests on the sea bottom. And big bones of great beasts. There were sacred places in the forests. And tracks, leading from one to another, scored deep in the ocean bed. But now the sea level is rising. Global warming. The polar ice melting. In another thirty years many of those islands – Muckle Burra is one – they will all be under water.'

'So then all the poison will be washed off the island?'

'Perhaps,' said Gran. 'But nobody living there. Only ghosts.' She paused, then said, 'I wonder what the ghosts think when the sea covers their sacred places?'

While Lu-Lyn dances in her imagined forests the music starts to give nervous hints that there is something wrong – maybe it is far away but it's coming closer, better watch out, better be on your guard, better make tracks for home . . .

Lu-Lyn picks up her invisible flowers – or mushrooms, or whatever they are – glances nervously over her shoulder and starts along the homeward track, which zigzags to and fro across the stage.

Then she looks back and sees *it*.

Dropping her treasures to the ground, her hands go up in the air, while the music, which has been drumming and pounding closer and closer, like a grizzly bear, like a dinosaur on the warpath, lets out that terrific shriek. We've had hints of it before, but not the real thing.

Then Lu-Lyn, facing the huge terror – whatever it is – takes her three frantic leaps backward, crossing the whole of the stage.

And at the top of the third leap the Whatever-it-is makes a snatch at her, so she appears to be caught in mid-leap, so that she falls dead to the ground.

She wanted me to make chalk marks on the floorboards, so she would know to leave the ground at the right spot. She was to 'fall dead' just at the side of the stage.

'Won't the marks be rubbed off between now and the night?' I objected.

'Of course they will, stupid! But you must measure today where they are to come, and then mark them for me again on the night. Write it down. I've brought a notebook.'

So I marked and measured . . .

Lu-Lyn got me to put on the tape again and

again and went through her routine several times. And I sat in my wheelchair thinking about a poisoned island and about stone forests under the sea. At last it was too dark to go on.

I said, 'You'll fall off the edge of the stage unless we turn on some lights.'

'I don't want any more lights,' said Lu-Lyn. 'I've told Mr Alleyn I want the dimmest possible lights on the night.'

Mr Alleyn was the English master who looked after stage lighting and props.

While Lu-Lyn was changing back into outdoor shoes I thought I heard a sound from the coat rack.

'There's that noise again,' I said.

'Rubbish,' snapped Lu-Lyn, but she looked nervously behind her as we made for the door. I knew I heard something, though and, sure enough, as we got close to the entrance, a shadowy shape slunk out from behind the coat rack and put itself in our way. Lu-Lyn let out a gasp of fright – and I probably did too.

The figure was sobbing and snuffling and wringing its hands.

Did you ever read about a ghost they have in Scotland called the Bean-nighe? You find it by streams, washing clothes for dead people – shrouds – and it cries and weeps and whimpers

26

all the time it is doing its dismal laundry. And if it hears you and turns round and catches you, then you are done for. For then the shroud that it washes is *your* shroud. The shroud is for you.

I read about it in one of Gran's books, a collection of folk tales.

Well, this creepy character in our school hall reminded me of the Bean-nighe – but of course really it was only Mrs Bateman. I knew her because she used to be one of the dinner ladies at my first school, when I could still walk. She was Bry's mother.

'Oh, Miss Lynda, dear!' she says in a sobby, snuffly voice. 'Oh, Miss Lynda, my dear, please, *please*!'

And she grabs hold of Lu-Lyn's hands. If she'd really been the Bean-nighe, Lu-Lyn would have been a goner.

Lu-Lyn was very angry – I could tell from the sharpness of her voice. A voice she sometimes used on me.

'Who the jig are *you*?' she said. 'And what the shivers are you doing here? Let go of my hand, you snivelling old bag! Let me get by!'

But Mrs Bateman didn't. She hangs on to Lu-Lyn as if she was drowning in the river. And she gasps out, 'Oh, but please listen, please do! It's so terrible for the poor boy, so *terrible*! He was so active! Can't you please ask your grandma to take it off? To go blind at his age – at *his age*, Miss Lynda – it's not right! It's too cruel!'

'I don't know what you mean! Tell my grandma? What are you talking about, you daft old crow?' said Lu-Lyn angrily.

'Your grandma – Mrs Drummond! Everybody knows that she's got the power. She brought it with her from the island!'

'Power, what power?'

'The power to put the cold touch on somebody. Everybody knows that! And now she has put it on my Bryan and he can't see! He can't see! And that's too cruel on a young boy like him – *too cruel*!'

The wretched woman was crouching in front of Lu-Lyn, crying and gasping and shivering.

'Cruel?' said Lu-Lyn. 'Do you know what your Bryan did to my bird? And other things he's done? Anyway, my grandmother had nothing to do with what's happened to him – *nothing*! Now let go of me.'

'He'll never do it again – never!' wailed Mrs Bateman. 'He's as sorry as can be! We'll get you another bird. Won't you tell your grandma that?'

'I'm telling you, what happened to your son has *nothing to do* with my grandmother! Anything that has happened to him is his own fault. He'd better think about that. Now, will you *let* go!'

She gave a sharp twist to the woman's wrists, and Mrs Bateman let out a squawk.

Just at that moment we heard quick footsteps coming along the concrete path, someone walked through the outer door, and all the lights flashed on.

While we were still blinking in the sudden dazzle, an astonished voice said, 'What the *deuce* is going on here?'

It was Mr Alleyn, come to set up the stage for some parent-teacher business.

Lu-Lyn, cold as a jellyfish, told him, 'I think Mrs Bateman is ill. Would you like me to find the school nurse?'

'Yes, you'd better,' he said, looking at the crying, writhing figure. 'Here,' he told the woman, 'why don't you sit on one of these chairs for a minute? What you need is a nice cup of tea.'

We left him trying to compose her.

To my surprise, Lu-Lyn didn't go anywhere near the nurse's office but shoved my wheelchair in the direction of our bus stop.

'Aren't you going for Nurse?'

'Not likely. Why should I?' she said. 'Mr Alleyn can do what he likes with the silly woman.'

But I caught hold of a fourth-former who was

29

passing and said, 'Mr Alleyn wants Nurse right away in the hall.'

When we were on the bus, riding towards Chateau Mansions, I asked Lu-Lyn, 'What did that woman mean about Grandma? About the power to put the cold touch on? Why should she say everybody knows about it? What is the cold touch?'

'A lot of rubbish,' Lu-Lyn said. 'People make up these spiteful, crazy stories. It's all in their own minds.'

But I thought of that sheet of black paper. Which I had not posted. Which I had dropped in the river. I wondered if the cold touch would rebound back on me. I had read, in one of Gran's books, 'Beware of how you use the spell of the Evil Eye. For, once despatched, if it misses its mark, it may rebound on the sender or on any person close at hand.'

I remembered Gran and Lu-Lyn talking about Aunt Arbel, who had died at the age of twenty-five. And Lu-Lyn saying, 'Is the power always passed on? Is there always a girl in the family?'

What was the connection?

5

The Death

If Lu-Lyn and Gran talked about Mrs Bateman I didn't hear them.

I kept dreaming about waves slapping on a sandy beach. With a row of white houses behind. And lots of little creatures running, running into the sea.

Lu-Lyn was so tired with all her practising that she cried every night. Or perhaps it was homesickness. Even through a closed door I heard her. It seemed as if her dance, set in some long-ago forest, had stirred up old memories. Memories of a time before she was born, memories from other minds of other people in our family, who had lived long, long ago.

Did I say that the painter, Munch, who painted the Scream picture, *he* came from the northern parts, way up there among the rocks and mountains, where it is cold and dark for three-quarters of the year. People sleep longer than they do in the south. And dream more.

I'll tell you one thing about the north. There's a lot, a real lot of dark in it.

Three weeks went by, and now it was time for the school fête. In the afternoon there were races and athletics. Of course, in my wheelchair I didn't have any part in them.

In the evening it's time for plays, cabaret, dramatic turns and dancing.

Lu-Lyn's performance came about halfway through the evening shows, after some songs by a choral group. Before that she sat in the audience. Most people sat with their friends, but Lu-Lyn didn't have any friends.

She was too tied up in her dancing to have time for other people.

I sat with some of my mates, but halfway through the choral songs Benjy and I left the hall and went backstage. I had my chalk, and my measuring tape to mark out Lu-Lyn's three taking-off points.

Gran hadn't come to the cabaret. She never comes to school things. She likes time by herself.

Is she homesick for the island? Like Lu-Lyn? I don't know. But – like Lu-Lyn – she doesn't connect with people much at all. She lives in a different world most of the time.

Of course when Benjy and I went backstage we found a whole clutter of scenery and stage props and costumes and musical instruments ready for all the other people's gigs. I heard a kind of shuffling behind a big concert grand piano, but paid it no heed. There were plenty of other people about, on similar errands.

As soon as the choral group came off and the curtain went down Benjy pushed me on to the stage. I whipped out my measure and chalked the three crosses.

Then we left the stage and went back into the hall.

Lu-Lyn's music had started. Mr Alleyn had put on *The Banshee's Exile*.

The audience went quiet in a moment.

And when Lu-Lyn came on they went quieter still. Not a cough, not a snuffle. The spooky music sighed and sang and muttered, like the wind in pines, or in dry grasses on a cliff-top, and

Lu-Lyn did her solitary, carefree, meandering dance among the invisible trees. To and fro, to and fro, back and forth, picking make-believe flowers, dropping them in her imaginary basket. She seems happy, peaceful, relaxed, in the place where she wants to be.

Then the music begins to change and she hears something. A bit worried, she thinks it's time to head for home. Takes the familiar path and skips along it – going rather faster than usual, but still not exactly scared, just rather keen to leave the woods and get back to the village . . .

The music drums and flutters up and up, to a high point, and that's the moment when she looks back and sees *IT*. As the orchestra goes into its shriek her hands go up in utter horror.

And Lu-Lyn did her three terrific backward leaps, taking off from the cross I had marked for her.

The third was the highest of all, and at the top of it she really seemed to hesitate for a moment in mid-air, then crashed to the ground.

There was a moment's total silence in the hall. Followed, after a frozen pause, by a tremendous roar of applause. People thumped their feet on the ground, people stood up and shouted. I've never heard such clapping.

But Lu-Lyn huddled in a heap on the ground,

34

lay still, didn't stir. And I was puzzled because, when she was making her third leap, I thought I had seen her slip, and leave the floor a yard farther along than she should.

Now Mr Alleyn was kneeling by her and raised his hand for silence.

'I'm afraid there has been a serious accident,' he said. 'Lu-Lyn appears to have knocked herself unconscious. Could I have a couple of helpers, please, and a stretcher.'

People bustled on to the stage. Benjy and I left the hall in a hurry to go home and tell Gran what had happened. She won't have a phone in the flat. 'Why not?' I once asked. 'The airwaves it makes,' she said, 'might prevent my hearing a sound I'm listening for.'

Lu-Lyn was taken directly to St Martha's Hospital, so Gran and I followed her there in a taxi.

We had to sit outside a room where there was a lot of activity, people dashing to and fro in white coats with tubes and basins and electrical appliances.

None of it was any use.

After a couple of hours a sad, serious man came out to tell Gran that Lu-Lyn had broken her back and had died without recovering consciousness.

6

The Grave

Next day two things happened.

First, Mr Innes, the headmaster, came to call. He had been shocked to his roots, he said, to hear of Lu-Lyn's death. He came to express his condolences, such a tragic waste of such a tremendously promising young life. He brought with him a leather box containing the silver chain which Lu-Lyn would have won for her performance if she had been alive to receive it. Or rather, he explained carefully, if she had been alive she would have won the free term's tuition at the drama school – but, as matters were, that award had gone to Jocelyn Duffy for her singing.

But he hoped that the silver chain would be a reminder, a sad but important reminder, he interrupted himself to add, a poignant reminder of a talented young life brought to an untimely close, grievously cut short—

'I'll bury the chain with her,' Gran said briefly. Sometimes she sounded very like Lu-Lyn. 'And, Mr Innes, what's this I hear about a patch of grease on the stage?'

He turned pale with annoyance.

'Oh, good heavens, has that silly tale got here already? I assure you, my dear lady—'

You could see that he had been within an inch of calling Gran 'my good woman' but was able to stop himself just in time. 'My dear lady, I hope that you are not going to pay the slightest attention to such foolish gossip, spread abroad, I've no doubt at all, by spiteful sensation-mongers—'

'I'd hardly call my grandson a sensation-monger,' said Gran, colder and dryer than the east wind. 'He saw the patch of grease himself when he went down to the hall to fetch my granddaughter's things.'

Not only had I seen the patch of oil, the size of a doormat, spread over my third marker-cross; but I had seen the two-litre cooking-oil container casually dumped backstage behind the grand piano. Somebody had probably planned to come back and pick it up later, but had not been able to because of all the commotion.

At the funeral there was only Gran and me, Gran with a grim, set face like a tombstone covered in black ice. Not another soul, except for the man who read the words.

What did Gran feel about Lu-Lyn's death?

I truly did not know.

She was like a closed box, a shut book.

At night she walked in her room, up and down, up and down. I don't think she slept at all.

Sometimes she gave me a queer, puzzled, gloomy look as if she were measuring me for a suit of clothes which she was pretty sure were not going to fit . . .

Had those boys been responsible for Lu-Lyn's death?

The day before the funeral I had suggested to Gran that we should have Lu-Lyn's banshee music played, maybe she would have liked that. But Gran said no to that idea, very short and sharp. Wouldn't be suitable, she said.

So Gran and I sat side by side on the bench in the crematorium chapel while the man read the words. And then he told us that we could come back in a week to pick up Lu-Lyn's ashes. By then, he said, they'd have a place ready for Lu-Lyn in the children's corner of the cemetery.

After that we caught the bus back to Chateau Mansions. My wheelchair folds up and goes in the luggage place.

I forgot to mention the flowers. There were *hundreds* of bunches. Wreaths, crosses, sheaves, bouquets. They were lying along both sides of the path that led up to the chapel – with Kind Remembrances, with Deepest Sympathy, with condolences, with commiserations. From school, from neighbours we didn't know, from heaven knew who . . .

Gran had the lot sent to St Martha's Hospital.

Next week we went back for the ashes – which came in a lumpy plastic casket, tinted up to look like mahogany. Which it didn't. And this we took to the children's corner of the graveyard, where a place had already been prepared for Lu-Lyn.

Gran glanced round the plot, which was about the size of a tennis court.

'Hmm,' she remarked. 'Doesn't seem particularly appropriate for my granddaughter.'

Her face was set like a rock. What lay beneath the surface, who could guess?

The Kiddies' Korner of the graveyard – as it was named in the local paper – was all stuck about with plastic teddy bears, with pink and yellow flowers – ninety per cent of them plastic too – with the sort of little whirly windmills on sticks that small kids are encouraged to run along the park paths clutching, and which cause plenty of scars on face and stomach. There were garden gnomes and fairy wands, imitation birthday cakes and gift-wrapped parcels, fairy queens' crowns and spangled wings, there were pink parasols to keep graves dry, or shady, bottles of fizzy drinks and lots of poems and letters in plastic cases to keep *them* dry.

Lu-Lyn's grave – after we had put the casket in it, which also contained the silver chain Mr Innes gave Gran, after it had had four thick pieces of bright-green artificial turf laid over it – looked pretty plain and bare. Compared to all those other fancy decorations and gifts.

Much to my surprise Gran brought out three night-lights, which she had in her big handbag, set them in a row on the grave, and lit them.

Looking up she caught my eye and said gruffly, 'Lu always did hate the dark.'

It was the first sign I had seen which showed that she missed her granddaughter.

That night I had a queer dream.

I was on the motorway where, five years ago, Mum and Dad met their sudden and unlooked-for end, under the wheels of a monster articulated lorry.

I had blacked that day out of my memory as much as I possibly could; never thought of it on purpose. But sometimes in dreams it would come back.

In this dream I knew the road, knew that it was the one, yet there were no vehicles on it. Whereas, on the day of the crash, it had been packed with holidaymakers coming home, and with trucks and lorries impatient at all this extra traffic.

Far off in the distance the empty road stretched, for five or ten miles both ways, straight and flat as a ruler, with not a vehicle in sight.

'Why is the road so empty?' I asked Lu-Lyn, who was sitting sulking in the back at my side.

She said a strange thing: 'It's the path of power. From the runes of the past to the science of the future. A ley line from magic to physics. This was the way they had to go when they were driven out.'

'Who had to go? Who were driven?'

'The enemy. The vermin.'

Dad was driving the car faster and faster.

Lu-Lyn clenched her hands. She said, 'Dad! You must turn round and go back! If you don't turn and go the other way I shall scream.'

'How can I turn on the motorway?' said Dad.

'Have some sense, girl. Besides, we have to get home.'

'I shall scream!' said Lu-Lyn. Then she looked past me, over my shoulder, and suddenly her face went blank with shock, her jaw dropped, her mouth and eyes opened wide.

Something dreadful, something she hadn't at all expected, was just ahead.

Lu-Lyn screamed.

And her scream woke me. Only it was not her scream, it was the Edvard Munch alarm clock which somebody had wound and set.

They had wound and set it for two a.m.

Gran came hurriedly limping out of her room, wrapped in her old red woollen robe.

'Did you set that alarm?' she snapped.

'No, I most certainly didn't!'

She glared at me and I glared right back. Would I do such an idiotic thing? Of course I wouldn't! But I could see she only half believed me. Perhaps she thought I walked in my sleep (how could I though?) or had wound up the alarm clock in some kind of mental blackout. Anyway, Gran took the clock back to her room when she returned to bed. And for the rest of the night I lay awake, thrashing and tossing, and thought about Lu-Lyn letting out that piercing scream behind Dad's ear in the car.

Next morning the doorbell startled us as we were picking at a meagre breakfast, neither of us at all hungry.

The person Gran buzzed in was a policeman. Sergeant Davies. I knew him, as he had given lectures at school.

He said, 'I'm sorry to have to tell you this, Mrs Drummond, but vandals last night made a right mess of the kids' graveyard. And your grand-daughter's grave has been – er – mis-used.'

How can you mis-use a grave? I wondered.

'You mean you want me to come and look at it?' said Gran in a wholly discouraging voice.

'Er – yes, ma'am, if you'd be so kind. I'm sorry to have to ask you. It's not a pleasant thing to have to do . . .'

Sergeant Davies drove us both to the cemetery in his cop car.

The top right-hand corner, where children are buried, was a real mess.

All the little windmill-sticks had been pulled up and broken and their tops torn off. The plastic flowers had been trampled into the earth, and the gnomes smashed to bits. The birthday cakes and umbrellas and gifts and bottles of fizzy drink had been broken and trampled and thrown about. Garbage from the litter bins had been scattered.

The turf had been pulled from the top of

Lu-Lyn's grave and the grave itself dug up. The casket had been opened and the lid forced off.

'Is there anything missing from the casket?' Sergeant Davies wanted to know.

'Yes . . . a silver chain,' Gran told him in a flat, dry voice.

Surprisingly, the ashes themselves, which were contained in a thick plastic envelope, had not been touched.

'Perhaps they were interrupted,' Gran said.

Mr Burbage, the warden of the cemetery, and lots of other people, parents of children buried there, were now arriving, all exclaiming in shock and outrage.

'*Look at that*!'

'Did you ever see such a—'

'Quite disgusting!'

'I shall write to our MP, to the Mayor, to the Bishop, to the papers—'

'It must not be tolerated—'

Mr Burbage almost tied himself in knots, apologizing to Gran, promising that a new casket should be supplied, that it would be re-interred in the shortest possible time, that the turf would be re-laid, the night-lights replaced (they were nowhere to be seen) . . .

'What about the silver chain?' said Gran, dry as gunpowder.

44

'I wouldn't know,' he said. 'If there was one, that would be a matter for the police.'

I could see that he didn't like Gran and she didn't like him. And I noticed, also, that the rest of the angry, upset parents and relatives seemed to be keeping their distance from us – they talked to each other in low, shocked voices, and compared notes and condoled about damages, but very few people seemed to wish to share *our* dismay and disgust.

After the sergeant had driven us back to Chateau Mansions I asked Gran why she thought this was.

'Perhaps they are blaming us,' she said.

'But why?'

'None of these outrages have happened before. Only now, the day after your sister was buried there. Perhaps they think that she is the cause . . .'

I noticed a difference at school too. All my friends seemed to be busy somewhere else these days, they weren't around as much as they used to be. Benjy, who used to push my wheelchair to school said he couldn't manage it any more, he had to practise his violin, so Gran had to pay someone from Youth Concern to come and do it every day.

Gran was very quiet and tight-faced at this time. She didn't talk to me much.

One thing she did say was, 'I can't decide what to do with Lu-Lyn's things.'

That surprised me. It was very unlike Gran not to know her own mind.

Lu-Lyn's things, her clothes, all her ballet books, her costume, and her black dancing shoes that she used for The Scream, the tape recorder, and the tape of *The Banshee's Exile*, were still in her room.

'You could give them to a thrift shop?' I suggested doubtfully.

But Gran said, 'No. No, I don't want to do that.'

Then the phone rang, a few days later, and it was the police to say that the graveyard had been desecrated again. Worse, this time. Worse things had been done.

This time, Gran said she didn't want to go and look. What was the point? Let the police do what they could to discover who did it, and Mr Burbage do what *he* could to tidy up the mess.

But Mr Burbage presently came to call, pale, embarrassed and angry, carrying a wrapped package.

'I'm very sorry to have to say this, Madam,' – he didn't *sound* sorry, he sounded hostile and furious – '*very* sorry but the other – er – clients of the cemetery have instructed me to request that your granddaughter's ashes be removed from the plot and re-interred elsewhere.'

'Why?' snapped Gran.

'It is only since her – since her interment that these disgraceful acts of vandalism have taken place.'

'Do you think *we* did those things?' said Gran, very angry. 'Or do you think my granddaughter's ghost came back and did it?'

This startled and shocked Mr Burbage.

'Certainly not, certainly *not*, madam! But, you see, the other – the other parents and relatives have come to me with this request and I can only pass it on to you. I don't *like* to be put in such a position, I assure you, madam.'

He laid his parcel gingerly on the table as if it contained something breakable.

'What do you suggest *I* do with it?' growled Gran.

'That is entirely up to you, madam. But,' he added, almost in spite of himself, it seemed, 'whatever you do, I would advise you to do it *very* privately, not to let anybody know anything about it.'

'Somebody caused my granddaughter's death,' said Gran. 'I'm sure you know that. I know it. Why should we have to behave as if *she* was the one who committed a crime?'

'I couldn't tell you that, madam,' said Mr Burbage, and snatched up his hat and left.

Gran sat still as a statue for a long time after he had gone.

Then I said, 'I know one place where Lu-Lyn would like to be. Perhaps under the big fir tree, with Henry.'

'Yes,' said Gran thoughtfully. 'Yes . . . perhaps she could. But not just yet . . .'

Winter had set in, very hard and cold. There was snow on the ground. Just now, it would be almost impossible to dig a deep hole, deep enough, and, even if one could, the traces of it, earth on the snow, would be there for everybody to see, probably for weeks afterward.

Christmas came and went, without any celebrations by us, and Lu-Lyn's ashes stayed on the mantelpiece, where Henry the pigeon once used to sit.

One thing I didn't like. We had very few Christmas cards, of course, because most of Gran's friends were dead, and my friends had taken off, but one envelope arrived with two pieces of plain black paper inside. They looked just like the two that Lu-Lyn had sent off to her enemies Mack and Orrin McGregor, who lived in our building. She had taken them upstairs and slipped them under doors, and this envelope arrived in the same way, slipped under the front door. No handwriting, no signatures.

I would very much have liked to drop those bits of paper in the river, as I had done with the one addressed to Bry Bateman, but it was the school holiday time, my Youth Concern helper was not available for pushing me to school every day. I was housebound, unless Gran took me out for an airing – which she was not at all eager to do.

And, in any case, *I* didn't want Mack and Orrin to go blind. They had not been *my* enemies.

Gran solved the problem – if it was a problem – by folding the two bits of black paper into darts; then she opened the window and skimmed them out into the wind, which was biting and fierce that day, straight from the North Pole.

Down below I could see Mack and Orrin starting off with skates over their shoulders. Probably going to Kelso Pond, where all the kids went at this time of year. (Those who could skate, that is to say.)

A queer thing happened later that day.

Gran had decided to polish the spoons and forks, a thing she does only once a year. She has a bottle of fluid she dunks them in, and she keeps the bottle on a shelf in a cupboard. On top of the same cupboard live tins of paint.

Whether she shook the cupboard, or a passing

truck shook the building, I can't tell – nothing of that sort seemed to happen – but, anyway, a massive ten-litre can of white paint somehow got dislodged from the top of the cupboard and toppled forward, right above Gran.

'GRAN!' I yelled, from the other side of the room, and she swiftly reared herself back. The paint tin missed her head by a fingernail's breadth and landed smack on her hand.

She fainted.

I managed to hitch myself across the room and wrap her hand in a dishcloth. Then, luckily, Mrs Enderby from the next-door flat arrived; she had heard the crash. She went back to her own place and phoned for an ambulance.

Gran had to go to hospital and have a broken finger set.

It wasn't till late that evening, when she was back home again, that we heard the ice had broken on Kelso Pond and quite a few skaters took a ducking, Mack and Orrin among them. Lucky they hadn't drowned.

7

The Pigeon

'All this has got to stop,' said Gran next day. 'It's like a sickness. Once it starts, if it has been used for wrong reasons it infects everyone around. Go up and knock on Mrs McGregor's door,' she told me, 'and ask if she has time to step down and have a word with me about Mack and Orrin.'

No problem about going up to the McGregors' flat. I roll myself along the passage and go up in the lift.

Unexpectedly, the door was open. And Mrs McGregor was not inside. But a couple of builders' workmen were, one looking out of the window, one studying the ceiling.

'Yon's where the damp gets in,' he said.

'Aye, ye can see.'

You could. There was a big brown patch. The McGregors' flat was the top one, under the roof.

The man who was looking out of the window shouted an order to an invisible someone down below.

I crossed the room in my wheelchair till I was beside him – as there was no Mrs McGregor to stop me tracking dust over the carpet – and took a look out.

Down below was one of those huge articulated trucks with a crane attached. As well as the driver there was a man sitting in the control saddle of the crane. At that moment he was manoeuvring the grab so as to pick up a pack of roofing slabs from the rear part of the truck. The claws of the crane scooped up a bundle of slabs as if they had been a pack of playing cards – but each of those slabs was at least ten metres long, and wide and thick in proportion.

Heaven knows how many tons the whole load of slabs must have weighed.

Then the crane began hoisting itself upward, undoing more and more silvery sections, which came sliding out of the body of the truck like a coiled snake unwinding. And the dangling claws – with their oblong freight – raised themselves up higher and higher. Now they were right outside Mrs McGregor's window. Now they were up above, out of sight.

'Dinna lay them down all together!' shouted the man at the window. 'I misdoubt the roof mightna take the weight. Lay them doon in a row, side by side.'

I heard a shrill voice from the roof. Mrs McGregor.

'Come away out of there, boys!' she was ordering. 'Come away at once, the both of ye!'

Of course I guessed at once what the scene up there must be. Mack and Orrin McGregor, attracted like pins to magnets by the builders' activities, were up on the roof, probably in hopes of being able to get their hands on the crane controls, or on its load, when the men's backs were turned – and do heaven knows what damage.

Mrs McGregor had gone up to prevent this, and also to tell the workmen where the rain came through.

I whizzed back across her carpet (mud and oatmeal squares) and went up in the lift to roof level.

Mrs McGregor saw me first.

'Och, heavens above!' she cried. 'Now look who's here!'

Mack and Orrin gave me glances bubbling over with verjuice. But they could do nothing with other people about. Two more workmen were up here, shouting advice to their mate on the crane.

'If those men weren't here, though,' the boys' looks said, 'we'd have you over the parapet, chair and all. Just you wait!'

The two men, concentrating on the crane and its load, had no time to spare for me or my wheelchair.

For something quite out of order and highly unexpected was happening twelve storeys down below, just above ground level.

A pigeon – at least it looked like a pigeon – was making a series of swooping attacks on the man sitting in the control seat of the crane.

A pigeon? But that was crazy! Pigeons are not aggressive. Not like that. Could it be Henry? No, of course it couldn't. Henry was dead and buried under the big fir tree.

The man in the control seat of the crane was ducking and jerking and covering his face – he had let go of the levers and wheels that guided his load up and down and sideways. As a result, the load of roofing slabs was swinging down from the roof again, closer and closer to the tree.

The people in the road below had all flung themselves flat in terror.

The crane clutch with its load of slabs was swinging in great curves alongside the wall of Chateau Mansions. If it changed its direction ever so little it would shatter countless windows and smash dozens of balconies.

It was dropping lower and lower. People in the park stared, horrified, as they saw this murderous weight boomerang back and forth, crazily out of control, only a football goal's height above ground.

Looking over the parapet I saw Gran come out on the little balcony where Lu-Lyn used to practise.

With a swift glance up and down she sized up the situation.

She had two things in her hands. One was a paper dart, which she skimmed down in the direction of the pigeon, who was still aggressively pouncing and diving at the crane operator. He, poor devil, had scrambled out of his seat and was huddled against the cab of the truck by his mate the driver.

Gran leaned over the parapet and shouted, but what she said went unheard. I could not catch her voice above the throb of the engine. But I could guess what she was saying, it made obvious sense:

turn off the truck motor, which powered the crane.

So then Gran used the second of the two objects she had carried out on to the balcony.

It was the little Munch cushion with the painted face on it. She gave it a sharp squeeze between her two hands. And at once it let out an ear-piercing screech. It was unbelievably loud – I had forgotten what a shattering yell it gave. (Since Lu-Lyn's death it had lived out of harm's way on a high shelf.)

Everybody heard it – the people on the ground and the people on the roof. Everyone looked towards Gran. And she, leaning over the balcony rail, shouted again to the truck driver:

'Turn off the motor!'

This time he heard her, nodded, crept back into his cab, and did so.

But what he did was just too late.

Too late, at least, for the fir tree that was the highest in the land.

With an almighty, splintering crash, the load of roofing slabs, at the end of its pendulum swing, smacked into the trunk of the fir tree and cut clean through it, as easily as a sparrow's beak nips through the stalk of a crocus.

The tree teetered for a moment on its stump, then, as the load swung back and slammed into

56

it again, it fell lengthways along the truck, mashing it. By the mercy of providence the driver had left his cab again after switching off the motor, or he would have been mashed too. And his mate, cowering against the side of the truck, was buried in a mass of spindly branches, but scrambled out in a minute or two, looking startled to death but unharmed.

Meanwhile, the pigeon, distracted from its attack on the crane operator, suddenly shot up to Gran's balcony and, with most unpigeonlike ferocity, dived at the Munch cushion, pecking and slashing, mauling, striking and gouging with beak and claws, until the cushion was reduced to rags and tatters and a pile of foam-rubber scraps.

Then it flew towards the estuary and the sea.

8

The Crossing

Gran, seeing me peering over the roof parapet, beckoned me to come back down to the flat.

'What about Mrs McGregor?' I called, but Gran shook her head.

'No use fetching her in at present,' she said, when I was back in the flat again. 'She has too much on her mind now.'

'Did that lot dig up Lu-Lyn's grave?'

'They meant to, I reckon,' said Gran, 'but I've a notion that when they got there . . .'

'When they got there?' I said as she paused.

'Lu-Lyn had taken matters into her own hands.'

'What *do* you mean, Gran?'

'And then – the tree,' Gran went on, talking to herself as much as to me. 'The tree. No sense in planning to bury Lu-Lyn's ashes under it now. That was a direct message.'

'A *message*? Gran? You mean – from Lu-Lyn?'

'Who else? The pigeon, the grave, the tree – it all hangs together. She doesn't want to be buried there. No – there is only one course to take as things are.'

'What's that, Gran?'

'Take her back to the island. Bury her on Muckle Burra.'

I expect my jaw dropped as far as the girl's in the Munch picture.

'But nobody's *allowed* there.'

'We'd go at night. I know a man with a boat who'd take me across.'

'But, Gran – the island is poisoned.'

'Och,' said Gran scornfully. 'Tales to frighten bairns! What fool is going to be scared of poison that's ten years old. Forbye,' – I noticed that whenever Gran started thinking about the island she lapsed more and more into the island way of talking – 'Forbye there's a wicked weather forecast for the island over the next three days – hundred-

and-fifty-mile-an-hour gales without e'er a break for seventy-two hours!'

She gave me a triumphant nod.

'Gran! You aren't planning to make the crossing in weather like that?'

'Nay,' she snapped, 'I'm not a born fool! But, after the gale like that, there's, whiles, a spell of flat calm – who should ken the weather in those parts better than one who's lived there all her life, and her parents, and their parents, afore? And I'll tell ye anither thing, David,' – it was the first time that I could remember in my whole life that Gran had ever addressed me by my name – usually it was 'boy' or 'lad' – 'I'll tell ye anither thing – if we cross on Tuesday, yon's Leap Year Day.'

'The twenty-ninth of February. So it is,' I remembered.

I noticed another thing. 'If *we* cross,' Gran had said. She intended me to go too? What possible use would I be?

'But what's so special about Leap Year Day?'

'Ach! Did ye not know? On Leap Year Day – because yon is a day fallen outside the regular calendar – all hurtful spells, all acts of malice, are set aside. Leap Year Day is outside all rules and governances. We'll go on Leap Year Day,' said Gran.

*

So, on Leap Year Evening Gran and I were on the harbour-front at Firthside, the port for Muckle Burra and the northern isles. Not without trouble and hindrances on our way. A careering sports car had pursued us and missed us by a finger's breadth, overtaking on the motorway; it flashed by us, skidded, and disappeared over the hard shoulder into the gloom.

'Young tearaways!' said our taxi driver in disgust. 'They'll break their own necks some day and good riddance. If they dinna break someone else's first!'

Thank goodness we saw no more of them. But their faces had been familiar. Mack and Orrin in a stolen car.

Then, when we reached Firthside and Gran began making inquiries for Geordie Brough, she had a lot of difficulty finding him, and had to trudge from end to end and from back to front of the shabby little port, pushing me in my wheel-chair; and I began to worry, first that we would never find him, and second that, even if we did, Gran would have run herself to the end of her strength and would never survive the crossing.

Her lips had gone very blue.

'I can stay here and wait on the harbourside, Gran,' I said. 'You don't need to push me everywhere.'

'Not likely!' she said. 'There's a wheen rough types hereabouts would think nothing of tipping ye into the harbour. Ye'll gang along with me and hold your whisht.'

At last we found Geordie in a tumbledown little beerhouse, The Caelidh, drinking fire-water with half a dozen whiskery old men.

He gave a little start when he recognized Gran and – when she beckoned – followed her, I thought, without much goodwill, into the dark alley outside.

'Gude guide us, mem! I never in the world thought to see *you* in these parts again, Mistress Drummond! I thocht ye were long gone to bide with your great kinfolk in the southland.'

'Not so far off, Geordie, that I canna come back when there is need. And there is need now – sore, pressing need. And you are the man that can help me.'

I saw a great unwillingness come over his face. His eyes darted from side to side, as if looking for some escape route. But at last he said rather glumly, 'What's your will, mem?'

'Do ye still have your boat, Geordie?'

'Aye,' he said reluctantly. 'I do, that. But she's as auld as I am and lets water terrible bad.'

'She'd be good enough, forbye, for a crossing to the island?'

His eyes shot up to her face.

'Mem! Ye'd not be so daft? Ye know 'tis clean agin the law? Not a soul – living or deid – may set foot on that island until the new century is ten winters auld. Or maybe 'tis twenty winters—'

'Never mind the winters, ye crossgrained old loon,' said Gran. 'And I don't plan to set foot on the island. Ye mind the little creek to eastwards of the Voe Bay? Ye mind the Kelpie's Ness and the Silkie's Cradle?'

'Aye, Mistress. I mind them. Who should mind them better than old Geordie? Winter and summer I have passed those markers more times than there's herring in a barrel.'

'Very well! I want you to ferry me – and my grandson here – across the water before tomorrow's dawn so that I can leave a – a – a thing in the Silkie's Cradle.'

'Afore tomorrow's dawn!' he gasped. 'Mem, what ye ask is clean out-of-this-world impossible. Look, will ye now, at the water!'

We had walked back towards the harbourside as they were talking and I was watching, in cold sick fascination, how huge white waves, bigger than houses, lifted themselves, one by one, and crashed down over the outer harbour-mole.

Not a sailor, not a fisher, was stirring. Their boats were snugly berthed in the inner harbour and they themselves safe at home or in pubs such as The Caelidh, taking it easy.

'The water will be calming,' said Gran with certainty. 'In two hours' time the Firth will be smooth as a millpond. Ye know ye can trust me so far, Geordie? Living in the southland I have not forgotten my old weather-learning so soon.'

'Aye, so,' he said dubiously. ''Tis un unco' risk though. An orra risk! If I did do it – and I'm no' making any promise, mind! – I'd want a fifty-pund ferry fee. And I'd want the siller paid over, in my hand, afore we ever set foot in the boat. And what kind o' deevil's contraption is *that*?' he demanded, pointing angrily at my wheelchair. 'I'll not have *yon* in my boat, not for thribble the fee. There's nae place for it!'

'Very well,' said Gran calmly.

I had gasped at the fee he demanded, but she had evidently come prepared for such a demand. She pulled out a wallet full of money.

'I'll see your boat, though, before I pay any fee,' she added, putting the wallet away again. So he took us along to see his boat, the *Bonny Mary*. I was no judge of a boat, had hardly ever been in one. It looked like a terrible old ruin to me, filled with muddles of rope and fish baskets and lobster pots and spikey-looking tools, but Gran gave it a careful inspection and said, 'Very good, Geordie!

Here's the fifty pounds now. Ye can take it home to your wife – if ye still have a wife?'

'Aye,' he said sourly, gruffly.

'Well! Give Maggie my regards, remind her of the shark – how I saved her – she'll no' have forgotten that! And we'll see ye back at the boat four hours before dawn; we'll wait here. I want to reach Burra by break of dawn.'

'How will ye get the lad into the boat?' Geordie was evidently not pleased at this plan.

'We'll manage. And when you come back bring a flask of tea with you!'

He stumped off – slowly, grudgingly, casting many glances behind him.

There was nobody else about on the waterfront this rainy, stormy evening. The wind blew. The harbour lights swung and sparkled. The wet cobbles glistened.

I wondered what was the mysterious favour that Gran had done Geordie Brough in the past, which made him feel obliged to help her now. Had she saved his life? It could not be much less. Something of the kind. What was that about the shark?

How were we ever going to get down into that boat, which at the moment floated ten feet below us?

But Gran said, 'The tide's coming in fast. And the wind is dropping.'

She was right. An hour later we were able to clamber straight across from the quayside into the *Bonny Mary*.

'You go sit in the cabin,' said Gran. 'I'll leave your wheelchair in the shelter. I doubt nobody's going to come out and steal it on a February night.'

Then, as she was pushing it away, she said something else. She said – I thought – 'You may not need it when you come back.'

Had I caught what she said correctly?

I clawed and wriggled my way into the boat's cabin – which was no more than a canopy-roofed area above the size of a kitchen table – and sat on an upturned box.

In a couple of minutes Gran returned.

'Gran?'

'Yes?'

I balked at the question I had really meant to ask and said instead, 'How long does the crossing take?'

'Four hours, with a favouring wind and tide. Much longer, in contrary weather.'

'So we should get to the island by dawn.'

In reply she simply grunted. I was reminded of Lu-Lyn.

Gran had brought on board a great armful of seaweed – there were huge heaps of it all across the dockside, flung over the breakwater by the storm – and now she fetched out from her carrier-bag the casket containing Lu-Lyn's ashes, and began wrapping it in seaweed and binding it with twine, until she had a ball about the size of a pillow.

To do this, she sat out in the stern of the boat, where there was light from the harbour lamps. And when she had finished she remained there, brooding, with her chin on her fists.

'Gran?'

'Go to sleep! Geordie won't be back for a great while yet.'

'Gran, why did they poison the island?'

'I've told ye. It was a scientific experiment, to see which things survived. Birds, beasts, plants. They didna ask the views of any folk living there – just told them to pack up sticks and go! *Superior* accommodation was offered elsewhere.' Gran's voice was loaded with sarcasm.

'Do you think the island is still poisoned?'

'I do not. My dreams tell me different. And this three-day blow – gales of a hundred-and-fifty, all that spray and spume and surf – I reckon that may well have rinsed the last bane and blight from

67

the plants and stones. For those that dare I reckon it will now be safe to go back.'

'But will they be allowed?'

'That we shall see! But times differ now from what they were. These days folk stand up for their rights more boldly.'

'Gran?'

'Well?'

'You had a job on the island, didn't you?'

'I did.'

'What were you? What was the job called?'

'I was the Ridder. When folk asked me, I rid their crofts of pests – rats, it would be mostly. Or mice. One time 'twas mink, swum over from Panna, where they'd a mink farm.' She sniffed with fine scorn. 'Killed all the puffins, those mink did. But I soon sorted them.'

'Do all the islands have a Ridder?'

'Many do. But in some the art is dying. 'Tis a pity . . .'

'Gran?'

'Well?'

'Why are you telling me all this now. Why not before?' was what I wanted to say. The words stuck in my throat. But Gran answered them unspoken.

'Why did I not speak to ye of these matters before?'

'Umm.'

'Mostly, the craft will be handed from mother to daughter. Or granddaughter. 'Tis in women's hands.'

'So it should have passed from you to Lu-Lyn.'

'Aye. But then – first – I had to leave the island. And that pulled all amiss. Lu-Lyn was born on the island, and when your father moved to Kirkbrae after she was born, it clogged her spirit. Turned her twistways.'

'Yes,' I said. 'It did that.'

'Then there was the accident.'

I remembered every minute of that ride. It was just before Gran's move to Kirkbrae, the last month she'd spent in her cottage on Muckle Burra. Lu-Lyn had gone to spend a week with her. When we went to fetch her in Dad's car, Lu-Lyn had raged and stormed.

'*Why* can't I go and live with Gran? Why, why?'

'She won't be there herself,' he said patiently. 'She only has one more week in that croft. Then she's moving to a flat in Kirkbrae. She'll be near us. You'll see her often.'

'It's not the same! It won't be the same!'

'No,' said Dad sighing. 'But it may be better. New things may happen.'

'I don't *want* new things. I want to go back *there* – *now*! I want to be with her that last week.'

69

'You can't do that,' Dad said. 'School, for one thing. And Gran's busy. She has a deal to do, with her move.'

'If I can't go back,' said Lu-Lyn, 'if you won't turn round and take me back now – this minute – I shall scream!'

'Scream away,' said Dad.

But Lu-Lyn's screams were something else. When she screamed, Dad lost his concentration fatally, just for a second – she was screaming right in his ear, don't forget – and the car went under an articulated truck.

When I came to, later, in hospital, Dad was dead and Mum was dead and I was told that, due to a spinal injury, I would never be able to command the use of my legs again.

Gran had moved to Kirkbrae and Lu-Lyn was living with her.

I would, too, as soon as I came out of hospital.

'Gran?'

'Well?'

'What happened to that silver necklace?'

'Mrs Bateman brought it back. Said she was sorry. Found it lying on the earth on the vandalized grave. Took it, but then felt bad about it. Said would we forgive her and her son. I said, forgiveness was no trouble, but forgiveness was no help with healing. He and his mates did leave the pool of oil. Lu-Lyn did die because of that. Done is done. A curse does not die away. In fact it grows, like an avalanche. If the sorrow came from Bry himself, then he may be healed. Or will learn to live with his trouble. As you have learned to live, Davey.'

'Gran?'

'Yes, Davey?'

'Will the craft – the power – be handed on to *me*, now?'

'It may be so. Things are telling me that it may. Despite the fact that ye are a lad.'

'What *is* it that frightens creatures? So that they run off into the sea? How does this happen?'

'All ask that,' said Gran. 'And the answer is, I don't know. I believe what happens is that you put into the creatures' minds the one thing they fear most in the world. Who knows what that may be? For mice, perhaps a cat. For rabbits, an eagle, for people, different things. So then they run. What do you fear most in the world, Davey?'

Something unknown – dark, powerful – perhaps the Wendigo, the great ghostly creature of the northern forests ... The Bean-nighe, washing my shroud. Some huge being from the lost continents of prehistory?

'I'm not sure, Gran.'

'Whatever it is, it's there, waiting. And that's what I have the power to make them see, when the moment comes. Perhaps it is what Lu-Lyn saw, when she took that last leap. Perhaps it is what all people see when they die?'

'Is that what you think?'

'We'll not ken that,' said Gran, 'till we come to our ain leave-taking. Who knows, it may not be so for all? Some may welcome what they see. But that is the power that you may have, Davey, when I'm gone.'

I shivered. Like the thump and boom of the great waves outside the harbour-mole, it seemed a greater power than could or should be controlled by any human.

But Gran seemed quite calm about it.

9

The Laird

Geordie Brough came back after long, cold hours of darkness, and handed over a flask of tea and a bundle of scones.

'Maggie sends her best respects.'

Then he grumpily set himself to starting the engine of the *Bonny Mary* and steering a carefully judged course between the lights of the twin piers. Gran watched him hard for ten minutes. After that, satisfied that he was sober, and had not lost his former skill, she came and sat by me under the canopy.

'My mother, my grandmother, her mother, her grandmother, going hundreds of years back, are all buried on the island,' she said. 'So it seems the best for Lu-Lyn. I've a notion that the island wants her back. That's why she pulled herself out of the grave.'

What about me? I wondered. I was not born on the island. Will it reject me? Will it be angry?

Gran echoed my thought. 'I dinna ken,' she said, 'if the island is fashed with me or if it wants me back. I am waiting to hear that.'

Once we were past the arms of the harbour and into the channel between the mainland and islands, we could feel the difference, but the sea was not so rough as I had expected. The waves had flattened, and the surface of the water looked like a huge silk quilt, inky black or steel blue, every patchwork square bigger than a giant's meadow, all of them at different levels and different angles. The *Bonny Mary* seemed to be feeling her way through them like a tiny blind mouse, groping slowly across an endless floor covered by rugs of different sizes and shapes, all in motion, all slipping about in different directions.

The sky above was clearing. Acres of brilliant dark blue showed between torn rags of black cloud, and there were more stars than I had ever seen before, blazing in the rifts between the clouds, which rushed across the upper sky from west to east. But down here at water level it was calm enough.

'Lucky the wind is up there, not down here,' said Gran. 'Crossing the Firth is not to be thought of when there's a west wind at water level.'

'Why is that, Gran?'

'It sets up a whirlpool. Black Tam's Pot. Any ship that gets pulled into that is lost for sure.'

'Aye, Black Tam's Pot,' said Geordie gloomily, spitting over the side as he manoeuvred *Bonny Mary* from one level of inky sea to another. 'Folk say it's so deep that it goes right through the waurld and comes out in Australee.'

'But there's a west wind up there now, blowing those clouds?' I suggested.

'Ah, wind up at that level has a different effect . . .'

That news reassured me. I looked ahead hopefully to see if the outline of Muckle Burra could yet be spotted in silhouette against the pale band of greenish light that lay across the northern horizon, but not a thing could I see, and yet the lights of the harbour we had left were now tiny, dwindled into the far distance.

We seemed to be in the huge middle of nowhere.

'You had best take a nap,' said Gran.

'Oh, no!'

But my eyes kept closing. At last I levered myself off the box and curled up on the damp bottom boards. Gran draped something over me, an oilskin.

I slept.

When I woke, it was to the sound of low voices; I felt I had been hearing them for a long time. Gran seemed to be giving Geordie a history of why we needed to travel to Muckle Burra on Leap Year Dawn.

'But why bring the lad?' he grumbled. 'And him in a wheelchair, forbye.'

Gran went into some lengthy, low-voiced explanation. She seemed to be defending herself – and my spirits sank very low. I felt I was nothing but a nuisance, a drag; what possible use could I be when we reached the island? Did Gran have some secret plan to go ashore? She must know there was no chance of taking me. Without my chair I could not move, except by dragging myself painfully along the ground – and I couldn't keep that up for long.

'The lass took a wrong turning,' said Gran, low-voiced to Geordie. 'I'm thinking her luck ran crossways against her. It's a black unchancy thing to use that power for your own purposes. That's no' how it was meant to be used. And I'm in fault maself – I should never have advised her.'

I coughed, to show them that I was awake, and Gran offered me a dram from the flask of tea, and one of Mrs Brough's scones. The tea was fortified with something that shot straight to one's fingertips, and the scones were solid, stuffed with juicy raisins.

'Look,' said Gran after a while. 'Ye can see the island now.'

I wriggled out into the cockpit and saw a whole row of inky-blue hills up against the turquoise-coloured band of light. The sky above us was still dark, but the number of stars in it was much reduced.

I could see my ally Venus though, still blazing with green lustre over to one side. And, out of habit, I fell into my old jingle:

Star light, star bright, last star I see tonight...
What should I wish? Rest and sweet dreams for Lu-Lyn? An easing of her cares for Gran? Something for myself?

In the end I whispered, 'You choose, Venus, you decide,' and, when next I looked at that patch of sky, Venus had vanished.

'Which of those hills is Burra?'

'Burra's a low-lying island. The higher mountains of Screigh and Unst behind are hiding its shape at present. Soon though you'll be able to see the Saddle.'

'What is the Saddle?'

'Just what it sounds like. A grassy curve between the two highest hills on Burra. Your sister loved it. It was her favourite place. You can lie in it and not see the sea. She used to roll from the top into the centre. She said it would be a grand place for skateboards.'

I was surprised. *Skateboards*? My sister Lu-Lyn? She never had a skateboard.

''Tis supposed to be an ancient burial ground of kings,' remarked Geordie disapprovingly.

Well, I thought, I don't reckon the ancient kings buried there would mind if their descendants rolled or tobogganed down the slope above their heads. And I felt suddenly sorry for Lu-Lyn. She never had much fun. I could remember her saying, of her three trips to the island, 'Those were the best weeks of my life.'

And she never got to go back there.

Well, she is going back there now.

Gran and Geordie were talking about other hazards of crossing the channel between the mainland and the islands.

'Whiles, there's the Laird.'

'What's the Laird?' I asked.

'A grand sight it is,' said Gran.

'It will come, sometimes, after a two- or three-day blow, the likes of what we've just had. Some water gets driven down into a narrow gully at the bottom of the channel, the wind keeps it there by pressure on the surface and then – 'tis said – if there's a pause in the wind's blowing or a lapse in its strength up comes this giant wave from the bottom of the Firth and rolls right along the channel from west to east. But I mean a *giant* wave – high as a five-storey house.'

'And the skirl of it!' said Gran. 'Like all the woe in the world.'

'I'd like to see that!' said I.

'Best seen from well inland.'

It was much lighter now. We came within view of a pleasant rounded bay, with the ruins of a dozen little houses at the back of its sandy beach, and a solid, stone-built jetty at one side.

I wondered which of the little houses had belonged to Gran. But something in her look stopped me from asking. They seemed neat and sad, in the dark clear light that comes just before sunrise.

Geordie Brough steered away from the bay, though, and headed *Bonny Mary* eastwards, keeping well out to sea from the rocky point.

'That point is the Kelpie's Ness,' Gran told me.

'Why the Kelpie's Ness?'

'I suppose somebody once saw a Kelpie there. Not in my time.'

'You never had to get rid of any Kelpies?'

'No,' said Gran gravely. 'And it is not a thing to joke about.'

I apologized. Kelpies are water-demons, very hostile to humans, very dangerous. Before the time of electricity, radio, motors, long-range missiles, aircraft, people thought seriously about such things.

Beyond the Kelpie's Ness – a ness is a headland – a narrow creek ran far back into the hillside. A splash of white, high up, showed where it began as a waterfall.

A second headland, making the eastern side of the creek, had a natural scooped-out hollow in the rock close to the end of the point; it was easy to see why it had its name of the Silkie's Cradle.

'There's a story about it,' said Gran. 'A man from the village came by here one night, and saw naked men and girls dancing. When they saw him, they quickly put on their sealskins and dived back into the water. But one girl was not quick enough; he grabbed her sealskin and would not let her have it back. So she had to marry him, and they had several children. But she was always homesick for the sea, and one day one of the children found her old silkie-skin where her husband had hidden it under a corn-bin. So she gladly put it on and dived into the creek and was never seen again as a human. But she used to come back at night to feed her last baby, and that was its cradle.'

'Is that a true tale, Gran?'

'As true as such tales ever are,' she said, laughing.

It occurred to me that it was the first time I had ever seen Gran laugh. Was that because she was so close to her old home?

'Look, Gran, I can see rabbits up on the hillside.'

'Aye, and a roe deer. Yon poison will have lost its potency, I reckon,' said Geordie. 'Right, now, mem! I'll edge in as close as I can to the rock and idle the motor – will ye be able to toss yon bundle into the hollow from here?'

'I'll give it a good try,' said Gran.

'Tie a line to it. Then, if ye miss the mark, first try, ye can haul back and throw again.'

Gran did so.

Geordie edged the boat as close as he dared to the rocky slope of the headland. The waves heaved us up and down. Gran, standing with her knee pressed against the gunwale and her lips tight together, hurled the seaweed-wrapped bundle towards the hollow in the rock.

Twice, she missed. The bundle fell short, rolling down the rocks and splashing into the water of the creek. Twice she dragged it back on board.

'Shall I have a try, Gran?' I suggested, but did not see how I could make anything but a poor hand at it from my huddled position on the bottom boards; and Gran shook her head.

'This is for me to do, boy,' she said. 'I owe it to your sister.'

She flung the bundle a third time, making a huge effort, and this time Lu-Lyn's ashes landed fair and square in the rocky basin. There was a puddle of water in the hollow, from rain or spray, and some splashed up.

'Weel done, Mistress!' called Geordie, and then suddenly his tone of approval changed to one of utter consternation. '*Save* us, mem, look yonder!'

With frantic haste he spun the *Bonny Mary* about in the narrow creek, and headed full speed for open water.

'Och, my soul,' said Gran. '*The Laird!*'

It was a blue-and-silver wave the size of a mountain. It came marching along the coast like a Roman army, pushing its way over rocks, headlands, islands. It made a noise, a kind of droning hiss, as it approached. A wild, keening noise, like the banshee's wail. It did not roll. It slid, as if some huge shoulder, submerged, was heaving the surface of the water along.

Geordie, experienced and canny, did not try to fight against the Laird, but angled his boat on a forty-five degree course to minimize the shock of the moment when the wave hit us.

All the sky vanished, there seemed to be nothing above but curving water.

Gran, who had been standing by the gunwale, was catapulted from the boat like a leaf in a gale. I saw her face of utter astonishment, mouth wide open, above me one moment; the next moment she was gone, flung, arms wide, into a wilderness of spray. It seemed that she *welcomed* the huge swell of sea, hugged it to her, as she had never hugged Lu-Lyn or me . . .

The *Bonny Mary* was full of water.

'*Bale*, boy, if ye wish to stay alive,' shouted Geordie, and threw me a round pan with a wooden handle.

I baled. Frantically I dipped, scooped and flung water. My efforts seemed puny to reduce what was in the boat, but I kept at it, one reason for my diligence being that I did not dare look about me. We were still climbing up this endless slope of sea. But what would happen when we reached the crest?

We never did reach it.

Due to Geordie's expert handling, the *Bonny Mary* sidled her way southerly across the immense wave as it travelled on eastwards; and at last it left us behind in mid-channel. 'And,' Geordie said grimly, 'fifteen miles tae eastward of our proper course.'

'But, Geordie – *what about Gran*?'

He blew out his cheeks and spread out his hands. 'Man, Davey, she'd not stand a chance! Nae more than a snowflake in Satan's kitchen. Not with a hundred thousand tons of water atop of her. Dinna grieve for your Gran, lad. 'Twas no' a bad way for her to go. A way she might even have chosen herself. To straighten out what had gone amiss.'

Working away at my baling I supposed he might be right. Gran must have been very glad that she had seen the island again. And that she had done what she intended with Lu-Lyn's ashes.

(Where were they now? Carried to the world's end on the Laird's shoulder? Or down in those fossil forests, among the bones of dinosaurs?)

The sun suddenly rose, bright as a bonfire, on the eastern horizon. To our north, Muckle Burra was shrugging back into its blue retinue of mountainous islands. Some of them, in the sun's rays, glittered white with snow.

Now I could see the Saddle, outlined against one of those white slopes. A good place for skateboards, Lu-Lyn had thought. How did she know that? She never had a skateboard.

If *I* ever went back to live on Muckle Burra I

would turn it into a friendly, welcoming place, with a golf course for summer visitors and a skateboard park for their children. The long months of winter would give enough time for the island to retire into its old silence and solitude.

'Ye'll be faring back to Muckle Burra, maybe?' inquired Geordie, catching my thought.

'If I can . . .'

Gran and Lu-Lyn, Mother and Dad were gone. All my family. I would have to learn to live with the aching emptiness of that. 'As you have learned to live, Davey,' I remembered Gran saying.

I laid the empty baling pan aside.

'Ye did a grand job there,' said Geordie. He went on, 'If ye went back, I ken half a dozen lads who'd not say no to the chance of setting up on their own. 'Twould be worth thinking about. Ye'd need to learn to handle a boat. 'Twould be worth thinking about,' he repeated.

I thought about it. The mainland came closer. The shabby grey buildings of Firthside stood out from their background. People were to be seen on the quay. Leap Year Day was just beginning.

I wondered if my wheelchair would still be in the shelter where Gran had left it.

When Geordie tied up against the inner pier the tide was still low. Fishing boats lay beached on their sides, scattered across the sandy harbour floor.

I looked up at the steep flight of granite steps that rose between our gunwale and the quay above. At high tide, when we went aboard, it had been possible to step straight across from the quayside into the boat.

'Ye'll need help up the steps, likely?' suggested Geordie.

'No,' I said. 'Thank you. I believe I can walk . . .'